THE CHILDREN'S CLASSICS Collection

Volume 2

Dados Internacionais de Catalogação na Publicação (CIP) de acordo com ISBD

T696t Twain, Mark.
The adventures of Huckleberry Finn / Mark Twain. - Jandira, SP : W. Books, 2025.
120 p. ; 12,80cm x 19,80cm - (Classics).

ISBN: 978-65-5294-117-6

1. Literatura americana. 2. Literatura estrangeira. 3. Clássicos. 4. Aventura.
5. História. I. Título. II. Série.

2025-2493 CDD 810
CDU 821.111-3

Elaborada por Lucio Feitosa - CRB-8/8803
Índice para catálogo sistemático:
1. Literatura americana 810
2. Literatura americana 821.111-3

Text based on the original story by Mark Twain,
adapted by Gemma Barder
Illustrations by Roberta Bordone

1st edition in 2025
www.cirandacultural.com.br

The Adventures of Huckleberry Finn

Mark Twain

W. Books

Hucklebery Finn

A thirteen-year-old boy

Widow Douglas

Huckleberry's guardian

Miss Watson

Widow Douglas's sister

Pap

Huckleberry's father

Tom Sawyer

Huckleberry's best friend

Judge Thatcher

A local judge

Jim

A slave

Mr Grangerford

Wealthy plantation owner

Mrs Grangerford

Mr Grangerford's wife

Buck Grangerford

One of the Grangerford sons

The Duke

A conman

The King

A conman

Mary Jane Wilkes

Eldest sister of a wealthy family

Uncle Silas

Tom's uncle

Aunt Sally

Tom's aunt

Aunt Polly

Tom's aunt

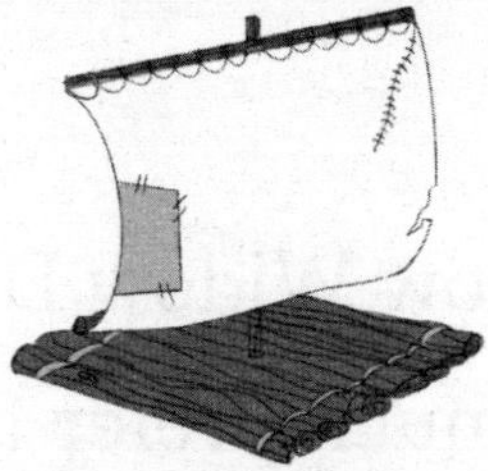

Chapter One

My name is Huckleberry Finn. I live in a real nice house in a town called St Petersburg, on the banks of the Mississippi River. I didn't always live in this house, wear fancy clothes, or go to school every day and church on Sundays. And, to tell you the truth, I'm not all that comfortable wearing smart shirts and proper shoes all the time.

St Petersburg
A fictional town made up for this story, in the real-life state of Missouri.

Mississippi River
The second longest river in the USA. It runs through ten states.

But that's how Widow Douglas likes it. I'd much prefer to be running wild in the woods and having adventures with my best friend, Tom Sawyer.

Widow Douglas takes care of me because I'm only thirteen and don't have Ma anymore. When Pap is in town, he wastes most of his time in the inn. So, Judge Thatcher agreed that it would be best for everyone if I go and live with the old widow and her sister, Miss Watson.

My new house is closer to Tom's now, unlike Pap's old shack in the woods. It means that he can call on me, throwing stones at my window, day or night. I lift up the window and shimmy down the drainpipe. These are the only times I can get out and have a little fun.

Widow Douglas is kind to me, but her sister can be bossy. Miss Watson looks at me like I'm always up to no good. Even though I get three meals a day and a warm room all to myself, I sometimes catch myself staring out of my window at the Mississippi.

Watching the sunlight bouncing off the water and the steamboats floating by, I sit and wonder if there is more to this life than smart clothes, reading, writing and praying.

Tom and I had just finished school one afternoon when we decided to go to our hideout down by the river. A few months ago, we'd discovered a huge pile of money. It had been the best adventure of our lives. Ever since then we'd been looking for another great adventure. Nothing had come close, yet.

steamboat
Passenger boats powered by steam. They typically had paddle wheels at the back.

‘Sometimes I wish I could just run away,’ I said to Tom, throwing stones from the riverbank and watching them skip across the water.

'Well, you can't,' Tom replied. 'If you left the widow's place, I couldn't call on you anymore.'

I sighed. It was different for Tom. He had always lived in a nice house. He was taken care of by his Aunt Polly and had a real family around him. He was my best friend, but I sometimes thought he didn't understand me.

Just as I was about to argue some more, I stopped still. There were clear footprints in the mud just down the bank from our hideout. On each heel of the footprint was a cross. I only knew one pair of boots that had a cross in them like that. Fear ripped through me like a storm. They were Pap's boots.

My father was back in town.

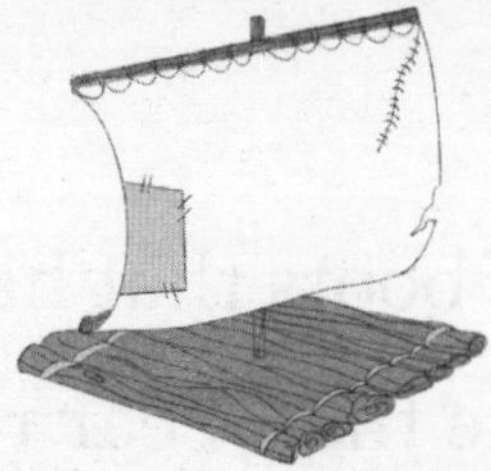

Chapter Two

If Pap was back in town that could only mean one thing. He must have heard about the money Tom and I had found. I knew as soon as they put it in the newspaper that Pap would come sooner or later to try to take the money from me.

You might wonder why my pap being back in town would make me so fearful. My pap isn't like most fathers. He never read me a bedtime story or kissed me goodnight. He was always too busy causing trouble or disappearing without a word.

I was scared when he was around because he would beat me.

I decided the best idea would be to get rid of my money. Then, just maybe, Pap would lose interest in me again.

I ran to Judge Thatcher's office in town and begged him to take the money off me.

'Now, now, Huckleberry,' the judge said with a kind smile playing across his lips. 'I can't just take your money. You found it, so it's yours.'

'If I have it, Pap will come and find me and try to take it from me!' I said.

The judge frowned and paced around his office. 'I'll tell you what,' he said. 'I will buy your fortune from you, for one dollar. When you are ready to have it again, you can buy it

back at the same price.'

I thought that was a mighty fair deal. I shook the judge's hand and, with relief washing over me, headed back to Widow Douglas's house for dinner.

Miss Watson and Widow Douglas's house was surrounded by farmland. They owned slaves who worked on the land and in the house. One of the slaves was a tall man called Jim, who always said hello to me. Jim also used to say he could see things regular people couldn't, like the future. Part of me didn't believe him. But part of me also wanted it to be true, so I could find out what was going to happen with my pap.

Instead of heading to the front porch when I got home from town, I made my way to the small, ramshackle cluster of huts where the slaves lived. I found Jim washing himself in a water trough.

'Jim, I need you to look into my future,' I said.

Jim looked hot and tired, but he smiled and beckoned me to follow him. 'What do you want to be looking into your future for?' asked Jim, sitting on a wooden chair outside his hut.

'I need to know if my pap is going to come and see me, and what he's going to do.'

Jim closed his eyes and breathed in the warm air. After a while, I wondered if he might have fallen asleep, but then his eyes opened wide and he began to speak.

'Your pap has two angels on his shoulders. One is good. It tells him the right way

to behave. The other angel is bad. It's the angel that your pap listens to when he gets into trouble. I can't tell which one of these angels is goin' to win this time. But what I do know is that you'll be all right, Huck.'

That was good enough for me, for now. I smiled and ran back to the house. I could smell meat and potatoes rising up from the kitchen downstairs, so I washed my hands and straightened my hair the way I knew Widow Douglas liked. The three of us ate dinner together and I made up all kinds of excuses as to why my clothes were dirty. I couldn't tell them I'd been playing by the river. Miss Watson wouldn't approve.

The worry of seeing Pap's boot prints, followed by the relief of selling my fortune to the judge, had made me real tired. I took a candle and headed to my room to sleep. As I set my candle on the little table by my bed, the room filled with light. And there, sitting by the open window, was Pap.

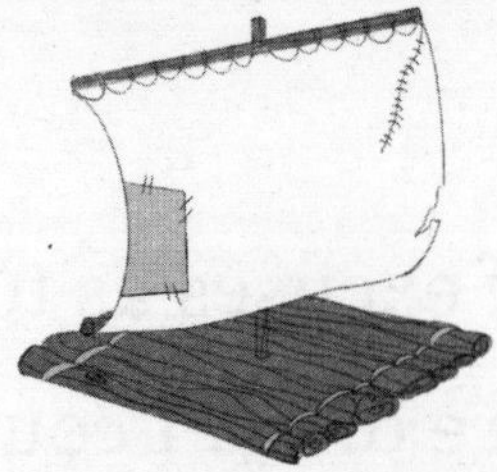

Chapter Three

I froze, rooted to the spot. I stared at Pap and he stared right back at me with a strange smile on his face. He looked worse than the last time I saw him. His hair was long and hung in black ropes around his pale face. His eyes were sunk back into his head and some of his teeth had fallen out.

'Ain't you pleased to see your old pap?' he said at last.

'Sure,' I replied, even though

it was probably the biggest lie I ever told.

'I came to congratulate you,' said Pap, standing up. 'I hear you're quite the big man here in town. And awfully rich, too.'

I backed as far as I could into the corner of my room as Pap slowly stepped towards me.

'N-not anymore,' I said, trying to steady my voice.

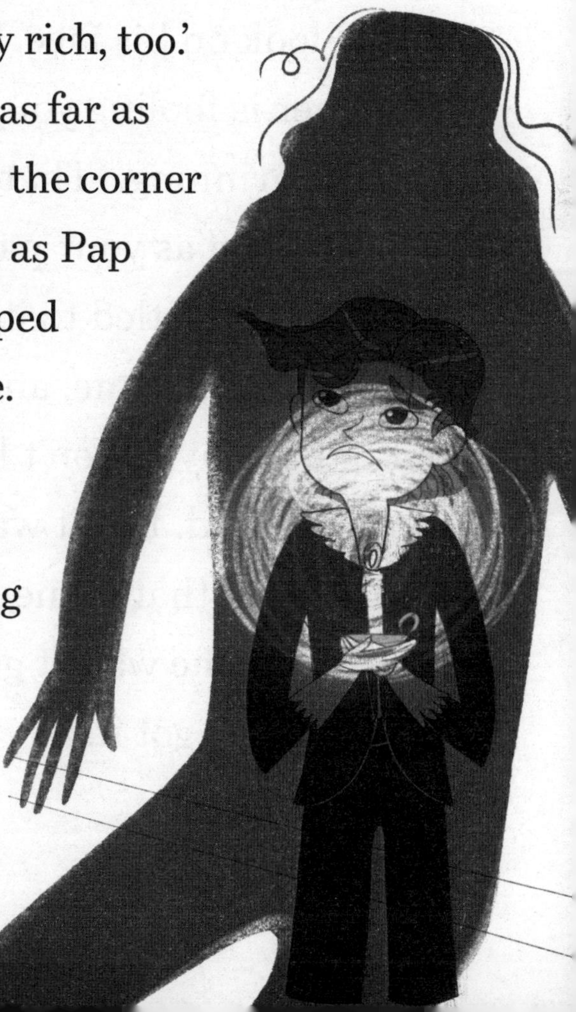

I didn't want to show Pap that I was afraid of him. 'I sold my fortune to the judge for a dollar.'

Pap burst into a horrible cackle that filled the room. He had a wild look on his face. 'Judge Thatcher is fooling you, son,' he said, grinning. 'That money is yours, and as your pap, that means I'm entitled to it.'

Pap lunged at me, and I dodged out of the way. 'I don't have it no more!' I cried. But it was no good. Pap wanted that money, and I knew that he wasn't going to stop until he got it.

'You're coming to live with me again,' he said, breathing heavily. 'No son of mine is going to waste his time reading, writing, praying and wearing fancy clothes.'

Pap grabbed me by the arm and swung me over his shoulder as though I weighed no more than a bag of flour. There was nothing Widow Douglas could do to stop him. Miss Watson even hit him a couple of times with her umbrella. But he was too strong for either of them.

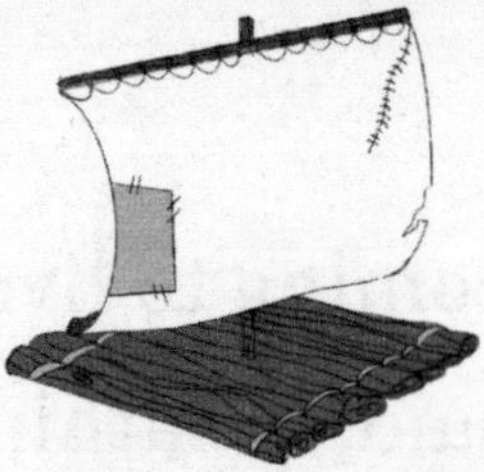

Chapter Four

Pap's shack in the woods was just one room. At one end was a black iron stove and an old crate with a tin plate and mug on top. At the other end was a pile of sacks and hay for sleeping on. It always felt damp, no matter the time of year or how hot the sun got. The floor was made of packed mud.

For the first few days I was there, Widow

Douglas and Judge Thatcher came by to try to take me back to town. But Pap was ready for them. He'd become friendly with another judge at one of the inns, who told him he had every right to keep me as long as he stayed in St Petersburg.

I stopped going to school. Instead, I spent my days hunting and fishing, which I didn't mind all too much. I missed spending time with Tom. But on the days when Pap wasn't around, I was mostly fine. It was the days and nights he came back moody that were the problem. Sometimes he was so angry he wouldn't even know who I was. He started to beat me again. Then there were days when he would lock me in the shack for hours on end.

Soon I said to myself, *Huck, this is no life*. I had to do something, so I hatched a plan. I knew that Pap was going to be away for a while. I waited until he had left and snuck the wood-chopping axe under my sack. As soon as he was far enough away from the shack, I chopped at the lock on the door.

I could have just run away

there and then, but I had to make sure Pap wouldn't follow me. The only way he would leave me alone is if he thought I was dead. So, I had to make him, and everyone else in town, think that was just what had happened.

I turned the crate over and threw the mug and plate around to make it look like there had been a fight. I took the axe and smeared it with the blood from a pig Pap had tied up outside. I even pulled out some of my own hair and stuck it to the bloody axe. When Pap came back, he would think I was a goner.

I grabbed the last chunk of bread and a flask of water from the hut and ran to the river. Pap's raft was tied up, so I took it and sailed over to Jackson Island as quickly as I could. My neck ached from looking back so often to see if I had been spotted.

Jackson Island was a place not many people visited if they could help it. It was thick with trees and I knew I could lay low while I figured out what to do next. Finally, I cut the strings of Pap's

raft
A floating platform used as a boat. They are usually made of wood.

raft so that it would break up and float in pieces down the river. I was free.

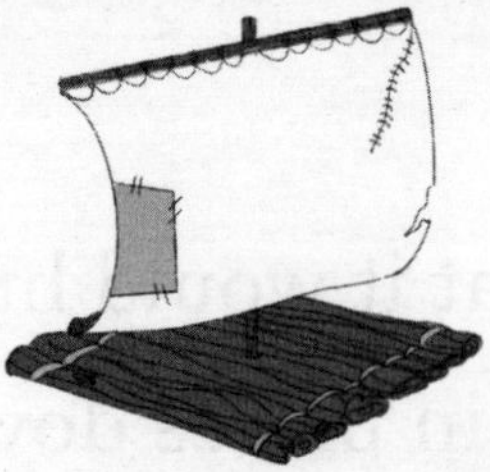

Chapter Five

For three whole days I lived the perfect life. I spent my time fishing, cooking on a campfire and sleeping under the stars. You might not believe it, but I found the woodland floor just as comfy as Widow Douglas's feather bed. Once or twice I had to hide from a grown-up who might have recognised me. But mostly it was just me and the river.

Then, one night, I spotted

another campfire. Someone was roasting fish from the river. I was terrified it might be Pap, but this man was taller. As I got closer I could see it was a familiar slave.

'Jim!' I cried.

Jim span round with a look of pure fear on his face. 'Huckleberry Finn?' he asked, as though he had seen a ghost. I soon realised that must have been just what he thought I was!

'Yes Jim, it's me,' I said. At that moment I realised how much I had missed seeing a friendly face.

'Everyone in town thinks you're

dead, Huckleberry!' Jim said, grasping me by the shoulders. For a second I feared Jim was going to take me back to town, but then I noticed his campfire again. It looked like Jim was hiding out, too.

'Jim, what are you doing out here? Why aren't you at Widow Douglas's place?'

Jim let go of my shoulders and looked down. 'I've run away, Huckleberry,' he said, quietly.

I was shocked. I had never heard of a slave running away before. I knew Jim would be in an awful lot of trouble if he got caught. 'What d'you want to do something like that for?' I asked.

Jim explained. 'I overheard Miss Watson saying she was going to sell me to a big house upstate. If I get sold, I won't see my wife or my family no more.'

Suddenly I understood. The slaves were the property of Miss Watson and Widow Douglas. It was up to them if they kept or sold them. It didn't matter to the owners that the slaves were married or had children. This was how it had always been in St Petersburg. But now I could see how terrible it must be for Jim.

'I'm making my way to Cairo in Illinois,' Jim said, a flicker of hope returning to his eyes. 'From there I can get a ship that will take me to the parts of America

Cairo
A town in the state of Illinois.

where slaves are free.'

I nodded. It was a good plan. As soon as Jim was a free man, he could earn enough money to come back to St Petersburg and free his family, too. As long as he wasn't caught before. It was going to be hard for a slave to make his way hundreds of miles down the Mississippi on his own. Someone was bound to notice him.

'How about I come with you?' I said, sitting down by Jim's fire and staring at the fish he had cooked for his supper. 'I'll help you get to Cairo.'

Jim beamed. He knew, just as I did, that if we were going to get away, we would be better off together.

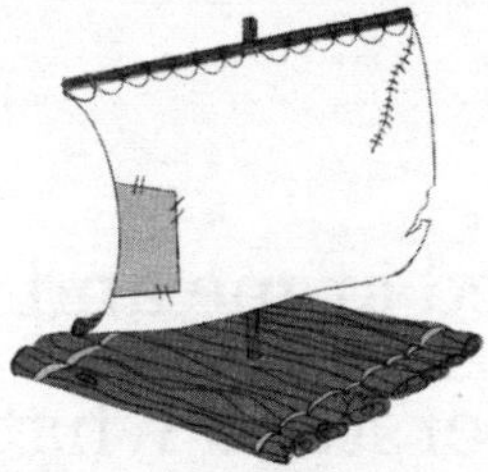

Chapter Six

The following day, the rain came. When the rain comes down hard by the Mississippi it means only one thing: a flood.

The river had risen as high as Jim's camp and washed away the small shelter he had made. We huddled under a tree and watched as capsized boats, trees and all sorts flowed down the river.

'Look!' I said, as I saw a sturdy canoe on its way towards us.

Jim looked at me and nodded that he understood what I was thinking. At the moment the canoe was about to pass us, I jumped and landed hard in the middle. Jim reached out his long arms and pulled the boat to the bank.

After the rain had settled, we took the canoe out. I told Jim to stay low, just in case anyone spotted us. The devastation of the flood was all around. Carts, boats and stripped-out trees bobbed in the murky water alongside us. Then we saw a very strange sight. A whole house was tilted to one side, washed into the river up to the second floor.

‘Have you ever seen such a thing?’ I asked.

‘We should take a look,’ said Jim. ‘There could be food inside.’

We tied the canoe to the side of the house and managed to

scramble through a window. The second floor of the house looked as though someone had just stepped out for a moment. The table and chairs were still upright and the beds were made up. If it hadn't been for the water lapping up the stairs, it could have been Tom's house.

Jim ran around each room, filling his bag with any food and money he could find. Suddenly, he cried out. It was a strange, frightened cry I ain't ever heard from any man before. I ran to where Jim was standing but he turned me round and marched me back to the window we had first climbed through.

'What is it Jim?' I asked, frightened. 'What's wrong?'

'N-nothin', replied Jim, hurrying me back into the canoe. 'I just think we've taken enough of these good people's bits and pieces.'

I knew there was something else, something Jim wasn't telling me. But I didn't push him. He seemed so frightened. Whatever it was that he had seen, it couldn't have been good.

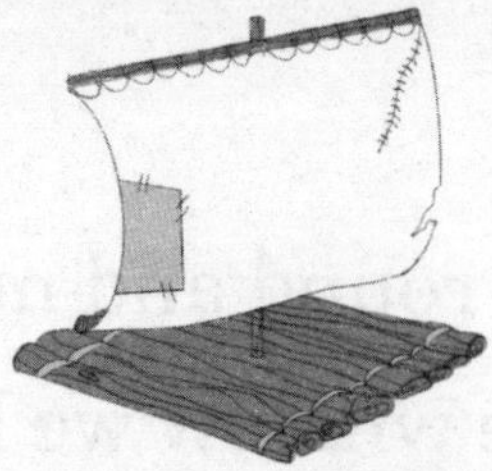

Chapter Seven

As the flood waters washed away, we gently sailed down the Mississippi. We stopped only at night to make camp. We swapped the canoe for a proper raft that we found bobbing in some reeds. Sometimes I would paddle while Jim rested. Sometimes he would paddle and I would let my hand trail in the water. Too much time doing nothing got me thinking. Tom always said I thought too much, and maybe he was right.

I started to think about whether what I was doing was the right thing. Widow Douglas had only ever tried to help me, and what had I done in return? I'd allowed her to think I was dead and now I was helping one of her slaves to escape. I liked Jim, but I felt guilty. It was against the law for a slave to run away from their owner.

As I was thinking, I noticed two men on the side of the river, staring at us. 'You!' one of the men shouted. He had a thick, red moustache and a cross-looking face. 'You two!

Come here this instant!'

Jim stood up straight and stared at me, wild-eyed. 'Should we ignore 'em?' Jim whispered. I shook my head.

'Best not,' I said. 'Let's go and see what they want.' Part of me wanted to tell the whole story to the men – well, the bit about Jim's escape anyway. At least then this feeling of guilt inside me would go away. I knew slavery wasn't right, but it was just the way things were.

The two men pulled our raft to the riverbank. The man with the moustache handed the rope to his companion – a huge man with muscles thicker than my waist. He looked past me and stared at Jim. Jim couldn't meet his eyes. He stared down at the raft and I could feel he was trying to make himself smaller – which was hard for a tall man like Jim.

But Jim knew that, as a slave, he was at the mercy of this white man. It was safer for him to look weak and powerless in front of this man, even though he could probably pick him up in one hand. I didn't like it. Jim was a nice man, and he didn't deserve to feel like this. He was kind, and he loved his family. That was more than I could say for a lot of folks that were 'free' to do what they wanted. Including my own pap.

'What are you fellas doing out here?' the man asked at last.

'Nothing,' I replied.

'What are you doing with that slave?' the man continued, staring at Jim again. 'There's been reports of a runaway back in St Petersburg. You know anything about that?'

I glanced at Jim, then back to the man. 'No sir,' I said. 'This here is my family's slave.'

The man did not look as though he believed us. Panic started to rise up in my chest. 'Is that so?' he said.

'Yes,' I said, suddenly coming up with a plan. 'We're on our way to the next town to fetch the doctor.' I started to cough. 'You see, my whole family has come down with the pox. Me and my slave are going for help.' I coughed again in

the direction of the man and his companion.

'The pox?!' the man shouted, grabbing the rope and throwing it back in the river. 'Well, you ain't passing it on to me! Get out of here!' With that, he pushed the raft with his boot and scrambled as far away from us as possible.

As soon as the men were out of sight, Jim and I jumped for joy and laughed. 'For a moment there, I thought you was goin' to hand me in, Huck.'

I stopped laughing. 'You're my friend. I want to help you.'

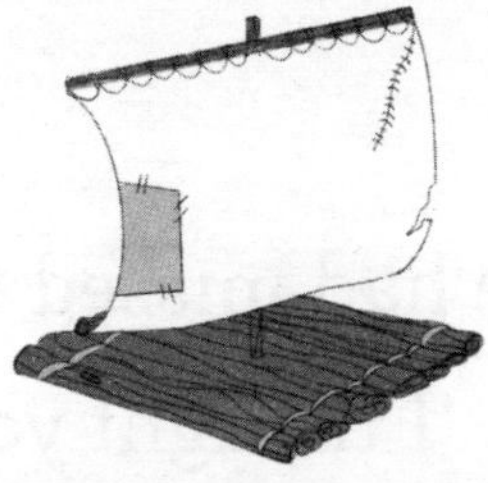

Chapter Eight

I'd never been this far down the Mississippi before. It started to widen up and the thick forest gave way to more houses and ports. 'We must be close to Cairo now ...' I said, staring out for any sign to tell us where we were.

'Cairo?' called an old man from a raft alongside us. 'I'm 'fraid you missed that a few miles back!'

Jim and I stared at each other. We had been floating for days and now we had missed Cairo all together. 'I thought you knew where you were going?' I said angrily to Jim.

'I do. I'm going to Cairo,' Jim replied. 'I never said I knew how to get there!'

I threw my hands in the air, but before I could argue some more, the shadow of a huge steamboat fell across the raft. There was no time to paddle out of the way. We had to jump!

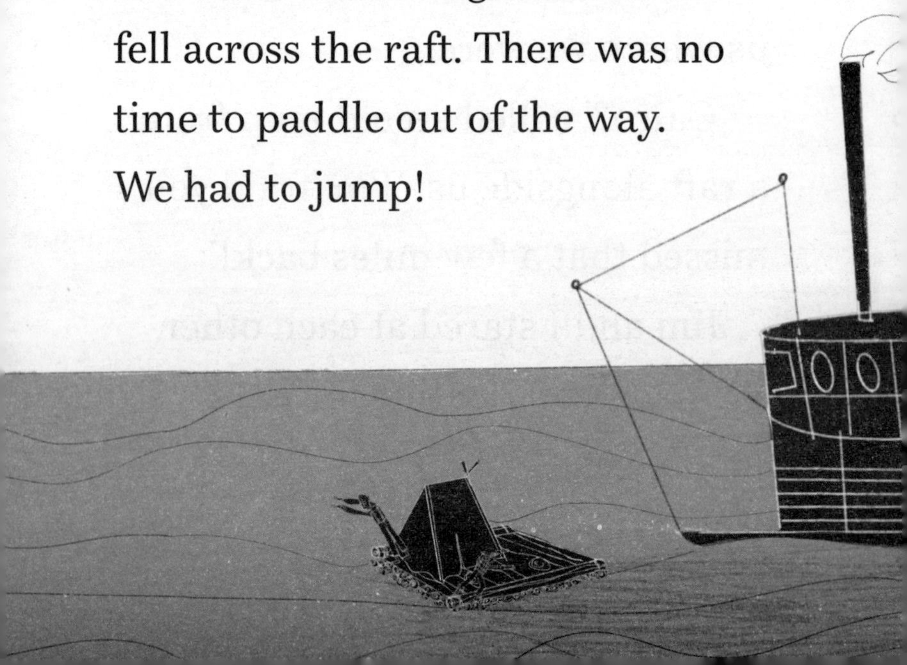

Coughing and spluttering, I pulled my way onto the muddy bank. I could swim just well enough to get myself to safety. I looked around but couldn't see Jim anywhere. I didn't know if slaves were taught to swim, or if he had even made it off the raft.

Suddenly, I was pulled up by my armpits by a man in a suit. He was standing with a woman wearing a dress so white and frilly, she looked just like a wedding cake.

'My goodness!' the lady said. 'Are you all right, young man?'

I nodded, still trying to catch my breath.

'Well, you must come home with us and clean yourself up. I'm Mrs Grangerford and this is Mr Grangerford of the Grangerford plantation.'

She stopped talking and I realised she was waiting for me to say something. 'Thank you,' I said at last. 'That would be mighty kind of you.'

The Grangerford plantation was a huge, white house surrounded by acres and acres of land. There were fields of cotton, orchards and a vineyard, too. Mrs Grangerford had me bathed and dressed in clothes that Widow Douglas could only dream of. When I was taken back to the drawing room, Mrs Granger cooed and clapped. She was surrounded by women in the same style of frilly dress, all in different colours.

'There now, don't you look better?' she said. 'Now, we need to set about finding your family.'

I'd got pretty good at lying over the last few weeks. So, I spun them a tale about how my parents were dead and I was living with a kindly aunt, and that my boat got turned over.

'We'll look after you for now,' said Mrs Grangerford. 'You have to meet my boy, he's about your age I would say – thirteen.' That's when I first met Buck Grangerford.

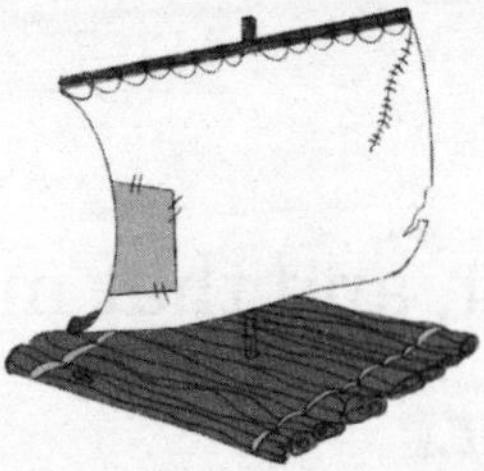

Chapter Nine

Even though we were the same age, Buck was taller than me, and he dressed like a grown-up. He had lots of brothers and sisters, so when I turned up, he couldn't wait to have a bit of fun.

I was quiet around him. I didn't know what had happened to Jim, or where I was going to end up next. Buck just thought I was shy. A few days after I arrived with the Grangerfords, he brought out one of his old guns. It was the best rifle I'd seen.

'You can have it, if you like,' said Buck, leading me out to his treehouse. 'I've got a shooting range set up in the garden. We can have a contest. We can pretend we are shooting Shepherdsons.'

Part of me wanted to take the gun and run away again, but another part of me wanted to play, just like I played with Tom back in St Petersburg. 'What are Shepherdsons?' I asked.

Buck laughed. 'Not "what", "who". They own the plantation next to ours and we hate them. Any time they come on to our property, we're allowed to shoot them. It's a feud.'

I nodded, not really understanding what a feud was but reckoning it must be pretty serious if they were allowed to kill each other.

'We can look out for runaway slaves, too,' said Buck. I froze in my tracks at these words.

'What do you mean?' I asked.

feud
A long-standing and nasty quarrel between people or persons.

‘I heard there’s a runaway slave in the woods, camping out,’ Buck said, starting to climb the ladder of his treehouse. ‘Some of our slaves have been feeding him, but Pa said he’s going to put a stop to that.’

It was Jim. It had to be. I was so happy he was alive that I couldn’t hide my grin. ‘So, when is your pa going to look for him?’ I asked, trying to sound uninterested.

‘Tomorrow morning,’ replied Buck. ‘There’s bound to be a reward for returning him to his owner, too!’

That evening, after supper on the biggest table I had seen in my life, I planned to take my gun and find Jim before Mr Grangerford did.

The Grangerfords had been kind to me, but I had to warn Jim before it was too late. I had just crept out on to the porch of the house when one of Buck's elder brothers came running up the steps with a letter in his hand.

'Ma! Pa!' he shouted. Soon the porch was filled with Grangerfords. 'Sophia has run off with Henry Shepherdson!'

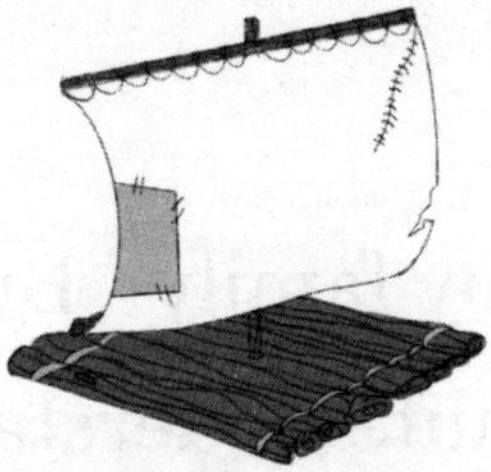

Chapter Ten

The whole Grangerford house suddenly filled with screams. Mrs Grangerford fainted. Sophia, one of her daughters, had run off to marry one of the sons of the Grangerfords' worst enemies. The men jumped on their horses and shot their guns into the air. I called out as I saw Buck running after his brothers. 'Buck! Are you going too?'

'Of course! I need to defend the

honour of my family!' Buck called.

I didn't quite understand what all the fuss was about. When two people got married in St Petersburg it was usually a happy time, even if the families didn't like each other.

With most of the family out trying to find Sophia, or kill Henry Shepherdson, I had my chance to find Jim. I ran down to the huts where the slaves were kept. At first, none of them wanted to talk to me. I guess they all thought I was working for Mr Grangerford. But as soon as I said my name, they all seemed to know who I was. Jim must have told them about me.

Jim had been hiding on the edge of the Grangerford estate, by the bank of the river. He had a cut on his head, but otherwise he looked just fine. 'I'm mighty glad to see you, Jim,' I said. 'I didn't know what had happened.'

Jim patted my shoulders. 'You look pretty smart, young Huckleberry,'

he said. 'You could make a nice home with those folks up in the big house.'

I shook my head. 'They're nice an' all,' I said, 'but I made you a promise, Jim. Let's get you to Cairo, if we can find a raft.'

Jim grinned. 'No need, I got one right here.' Jim stepped aside to reveal our raft, the one we had jumped from to escape the steamboat. 'It just needed a few repairs here and there. When I saw you get picked up by those fancy folks, I fished the raft out and followed you here.'

It felt good not to be abandoned. I'd like to think Jim felt the same way about me coming back to find him. 'I reckon it's time we moved on, Jim,' I said, smiling.

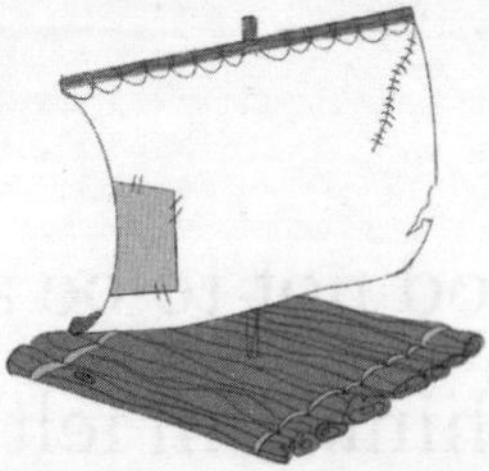

Chapter Eleven

We were back on the river once again. After we left the Grangerfords' place that day, I heard gunshots. Later, we heard that Buck and a few of his brothers had been killed in the fight over Sophia and Henry. I was upset about it. Buck was a good kid.

In fact, I was thinking about Buck when we first spotted the Duke and the King. They were running along the riverbank as fast as their legs would carry them – which wasn't very fast. They started hollering at us, asking for help. I knew the right thing to do would be to stop and help them, but I also knew we had lost so much time already.

'It's up to you, Huck,' shrugged Jim.

'I reckon we help,' I said, thinking how Buck had been kind to me, even though I'd only just met him.

The two men scrambled aboard with their carpet bags and we pushed away onto the river. 'Thank you, thank you!' said the taller man.

He had a thick black moustache, grey hair and wore a top hat on his head, though it was clear he wasn't that rich.

'Yes, most obliged I'm sure,' said the other man, who was shorter and rounder. He was clean-shaven and wore a bowler hat. He clung to his bag like he thought it was about to be stolen.

'If we'd have been caught, that would have been prison for us! My name is the King, and that is the Duke,' said the taller man.

'You royalty?' asked Jim, unconvinced. I could see him looking at the patches on the men's coats.

'We are, though we have fallen on hard times,' the King replied. 'You see, I am the direct descendant of Louis, King of France, and my friend is an English duke.'

Jim's eyes widened, but I wasn't at all convinced. 'Where can we take you?' I asked, thinking that if these men were wanted by the police, they might bring more trouble.

The King and the Duke looked at each other. 'Well, we might be in need of a bit more help from you fine fellows than just that,' smirked the king.

Something about this pair was starting to make me feel uneasy. 'What kind of help?' I questioned.

The king smiled the kind of smile that bullies use when they spot their next victim. 'Any kind of help we require,' he said. 'Or we might just stop at the next police station we come across to say that we've seen a runaway slave and his kidnapped boy sailing down the Mississippi.'

I felt like pushing those two fools off the raft there and then, but Jim held me back. 'We helped you!' I said furiously.

'And that was your first mistake,' said the Duke, resting his head on his bag. 'I wouldn't advise you to make any more.'

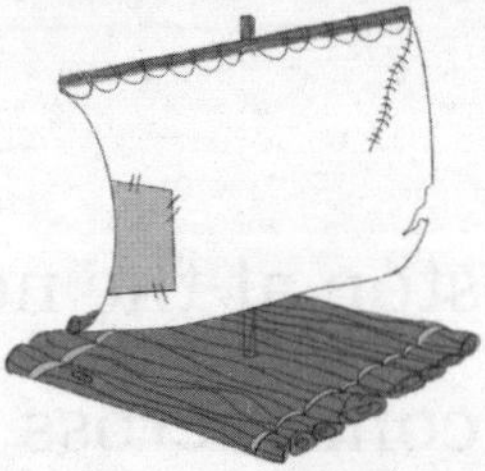

Chapter Twelve

Jim and I were well and truly stuck. The King and the Duke were older white men. They held all the power. No one would believe the word of a kid or a slave over them. For the next few days we paddled down the river for them, cooked

dinner and fetched them fresh water. If we didn't, we ran the risk of them handing Jim over to the police.

Soon we came across a small town with a port. We climbed off the raft to stretch our legs, and the King and the Duke went off to buy supplies. Jim and I were so hungry, living off whatever the King and Duke left.

We were just enjoying a moment of peace without the two conmen bossing us about, when they came running back towards the raft.

conmen

People who make their money by tricking people into giving up things of value.

'Right, you are my page,' said the King, nodding at me. Then he turned to Jim, 'And you are my servant from Africa.'

The Duke rummaged in his bag and pulled out a blue velvet suit that I was to put on. 'I ain't wearing this!' I cried, as Jim laughed.

It turned out that when the King and the Duke were buying supplies, they overheard talk that a wealthy man called Peter Wilkes had just died, leaving behind three daughters and no will for his possessions. Peter Wilkes's land and money was going to go to his two brothers in England, who he hadn't seen for thirty years. It didn't seem right to me, but to the King and the Duke, it was an opportunity.

They dragged Jim and me off the boat and asked passers-by for the directions to Wilkes's house. I noticed that they were putting on strange fake accents, which I guessed must be English.

The Wilkes' house was grand and old. It was smaller than the Grangerfords', but bigger than anything I could ever hope to live in.

Three young women stood on the porch. They were each dressed in black and their eyes were red from crying about their father. The King and the Duke greeted them, introducing themselves as their English uncles.

'Uncle Harvey? Uncle William? Is it really you?' said the eldest young lady. 'Can it be possible that we have never met before? And now we meet under such sad circumstances.'

‘We were so sorry to hear about our dear brother, but we are here to help. First, you must remind us of your names. Our dear brother was not very good at keeping us informed in his letters!’

The eldest daughter was called Mary Jane. She was pretty and talked kindly to Jim and me, even though we were supposed to be servants. I felt pretty sick watching the King and the Duke lie to this poor family.

Jim and I were sent to the servants’ quarters. We talked late into the night about trying to escape from that house. But I couldn't leave the sisters with these terrible conmen. I had to stop them.

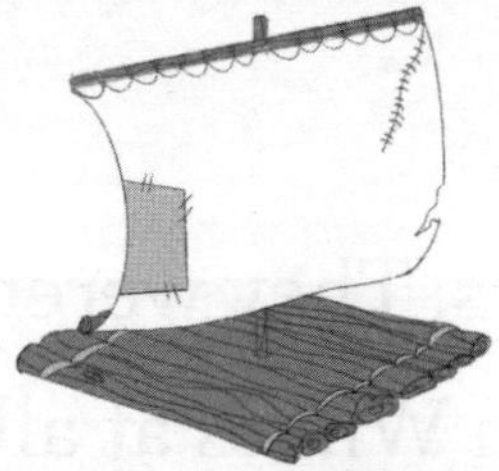

Chapter Thirteen

The next day, I was pretending to assist the King, when Mary Jane came in. 'I know it's not polite to talk about money, but Father had 6,000 dollars in gold,' she said. 'It's yours now, uncles, as well as the house.'

I could see the King and the Duke looking at each other greedily. They had hit the jackpot. I wanted to scream and shout that the money and the house wasn't theirs. They weren't Harvey and William Wilkes at all!

'I have an idea,' said the Duke. 'We should sell the house. Then, we can share what money we make for it. You and your sisters will never have to think of money again.'

'Yes!' agreed the King, sharing a wink with the Duke. 'Then you three girls can come and live in England with us!'

Mary Jane laughed and clapped her hands together in glee. 'England!

How magical!' She ran and threw her arms around the two imposters.

'It's not right, Jim,' I said. Jim was polishing the King's shoes with the least amount of effort he could put in. 'They are going to sell this house, take the money and leave those girls with nothing.'

Jim nodded. 'It ain't right, but what are we going to do? If we tell on them, they might tell on us. We're stuck.'

I shook my head. There had to be a way.

That night, I snuck into the King's room. He was snoring so loud, I could've tap-danced on his head and he still wouldn't have woken up. It took me a little while, but I found what I was looking for: Peter Wilkes's gold. The King had it in a little chest under his bed and the glow seemed to warm my face as I opened it up.

The money was mighty heavy, but I dragged the chest out of the room into the dark corridor. Now all I had to do was find somewhere to hide it. Somewhere the King and the Duke would never think to look. I took it to Peter Wilkes's room. The daughters couldn't bear anyone sleeping in there, so the room stayed perfectly made up. I lugged the chest onto the bed and covered it with pillows, then ran as fast as I could. It felt as though my heart might burst right through my stupid velvet outfit.

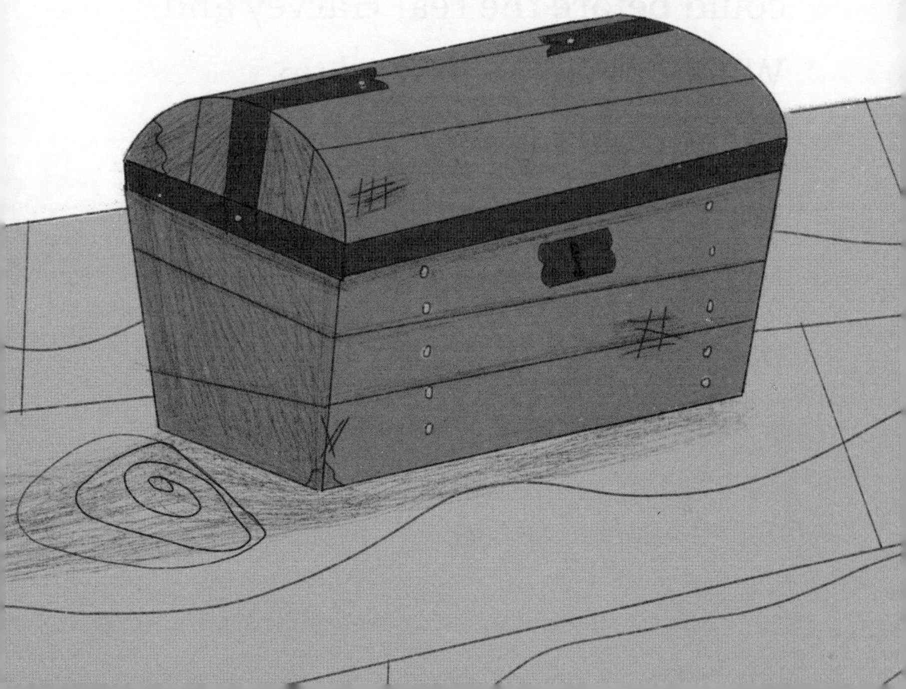

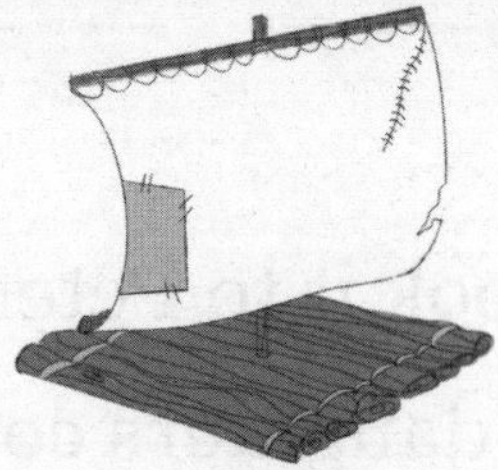

Chapter Fourteen

The following day was the day of the house auction. The King and the Duke were not wasting any time. They needed to sell the house and pocket as much money as they could before the real Harvey and William Wilkes showed up.

I ditched my silly blue suit and searched through the house for Mary Jane. I found her in the parlour, mighty upset. 'I'm so sorry, young man,' she said, sniffing and wiping her eyes. 'It's just, I am so attached to this house. I had such a happy childhood here.'

I felt sad then. I wondered what a happy childhood must feel like. Peter Wilkes must have been a real nice man.

'Oh well, I'm off on an adventure!' Mary Jane smiled, standing up and brushing off her dress.

'No, you're not,' I said. 'You won't be going to England because those men out there aren't your uncles.'

Mary Jane stared at me. 'I beg your pardon?' she said.

I sighed, the weight of everything I was about to tell her on my shoulders. Then, quickly, I let it all out. I told her who I was, who Jim was and, most importantly, who the King and the Duke really were. I asked her to leave some time before she let anyone else know the truth so that Jim and I could get away. Then, finally, I told her where I had hidden the money.

Mary Jane's body was tense as she looked at me. 'Thank you,

Huckleberry,' she said, slowly and quietly. 'You have done something so important for me. I shall never forget you.'

As soon as I'd spoken to Mary Jane, Jim and I left the house. We were soon tearing through the town on our way back to our raft, hoping it was still in the little port by the river. Jim cheered as he saw it bobbing in the water, not caring who heard him.

'We've done it, Jim, we've done it!' I said, untying the raft and starting to push away.

It was then that I felt the hot, clammy hand of the Duke on mine. 'Not so fast,' he said, lowering his weight onto the raft, followed swiftly by the King. 'We are coming too.'

'Paddle, you fool!' the King shouted at Jim.

I couldn't understand it. Mary Jane had promised she would leave us enough time to get away. The King and the Duke were out of breath, but they soon explained. As the house auction was about to start, the real Harvey and William Wilkes turned up. The King and the Duke had run away from the house just moments after Jim and me. We weren't free of these conmen yet.

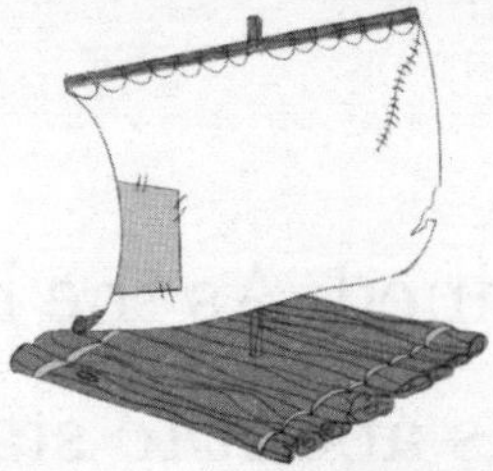

Chapter Fifteen

The King and the Duke had grown as tired of us as we had of them. We glared at each other as we floated down the river, unsure of what the other was thinking.

'Stop here,' growled the King.

Jim paddled the boat to the riverbank and all four of us got off. The King grabbed my arm

and pushed me against a tree. He had taken Buck's gun and was pressing it into Jim's back. 'Stay here and don't move,' he said to me. 'You follow us, you know what will happen.' He nodded towards the gun at Jim's back and I swallowed, hard.

The trouble is, I couldn't just leave them to march Jim off to who knows where. I'm pretty good at hiding, so I followed them anyway. I was

far enough behind to dart behind a tree if I needed to. They walked Jim down a track, towards a farm. The Duke got a tattered bit of paper out of his pocket and showed it to the farmer, who took Jim and shook the King and the Duke's hands.

Jim disappeared inside the farm and I stayed put, terrified the King and the Duke would turn back and see me. But they carried on down the road. I watched until they were just a speck on the horizon, and I am happy to tell you, I never saw those low-down excuses for men again.

Now, all I had to do was find

Jim. The sign on the farm's gate read 'Phelps's Farm'. It reminded me of something Tom Sawyer had told me once about his Aunt and Uncle Phelps who owned a farm downriver. If this was their farm, we might be saved.

I ran a hand through my messy hair before ringing the bell. A woman with corn-coloured hair answered and threw her arms wide. 'Tom! Is that you?' she hugged me so tight I couldn't breathe. Next, the man who had been talking to the King and the Duke appeared. 'Tom! I thought

you were arriving this evening!'

I stood silently, my brain trying to catch up. Tom's aunt and uncle thought that I was my best friend, Tom. I guessed they hadn't seen him in a while, and we did kind of look like each other.

'Yes,' I said at last. 'It's me. The steamboat got in early.'

Tom's aunt and uncle ushered me into the kitchen and gave me a plate of bread and jam. I was so hungry I nearly choked as I ate it.

When I finished, Tom's Uncle Silas told me how he had just been sold a runaway slave, and that he was going to take him back to St Petersburg to claim the reward.

'Where is the slave now?' I asked, as innocently as I could. 'Maybe I know him?'

'Oh, just tied up in the barn. He ain't going no place.'

I told Aunt Sally and Uncle Silas I was tired, so that I could go up to the first floor of the farmhouse and watch out for Tom arriving. Sure enough, a few hours later I saw Tom walking up the track to the farm.

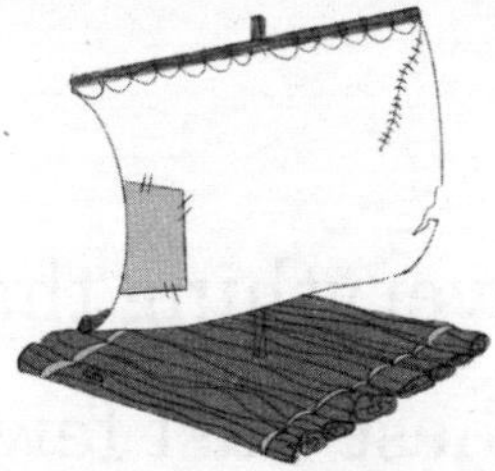

Chapter Sixteen

I ran out of the farmhouse before Tom's Aunt Sally and Uncle Silas could ask me where I was going. I had to get to Tom before he got to the farm.

Poor Tom looked horrified to see me. For a second, I completely forgot that for all Tom knew, I had been killed back in St Petersburg. Once he was absolutely certain I wasn't a ghost, and I had managed to explain everything that had happened these past few weeks, Tom let out a low whistle.

'Well, Huck, I sure am glad you're alive,' he said. 'Sounds like you've been having all the adventures without me!'

I shook my head. 'I'd gladly trade you some of those adventures, Tom. So, will you help me free Jim?' There was nothing Tom liked more than a plan, an adventure and having fun. All of which he was going to get if he helped me. Tom decided to pretend to be his brother, Sid, who had come to surprise Tom and his aunt and uncle. It wasn't hard to convince Aunt Sally and Uncle Silas. Tom and I knew each other just as well as brothers.

That night, we snuck out of the bedroom window, as we had done so many times before in St Petersburg. Jim was tied up in the barn with a flask of water and stale bread next to him. He looked utterly miserable. That was, until I tapped on the window.

'Huckleberry Finn!' he said, delighted. 'What're you doing here? How'd you find me?'

'You're my friend, Jim,' I said. 'I aint gonna leave you now, am I?'

It looked as though the door to the barn was secured with one lock. It was real easy to break through, if you knew just where to kick it. But Tom wasn't so sure. 'Where is the fun in that?' he said. 'Jim should dig a tunnel, or set fire to the barn, or we could ...'

'There isn't time!' I interrupted, annoyed. He was coming up with childish games, forgetting that this was Jim's life we were trying to save. It was Jim's freedom and freedom for his family, too. 'Help

me kick the door, it will be easier with two people,' I said.

But Tom was sulking. The adventure wasn't fun enough for him. So, I kicked the door myself. The door gave way after two or three good kicks and we ran in to untie Jim. I have to hand it to Tom, he's great with untying knots.

Then, the three of us were up and running. I didn't know why Tom ran with us. It was his aunt and uncle we were running from. He could have made up any old story and got away with it. But it was typical of Tom. For him, the running was all part of the fun.

And it was kind of exciting, feeling the night air on our faces as we ran like the wind away from the farm.

That's when we heard the first gunshot.

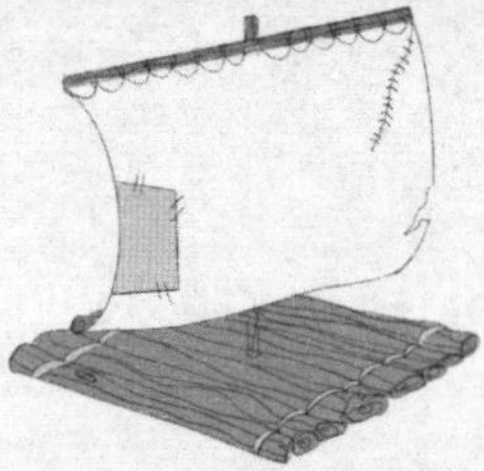

Chapter Seventeen

We must have woken Uncle Silas with all the kicking! I was angry with Tom. If he had helped me instead of sulking, we could have broken through that door with one kick, instead of the three or four it took me.

Another shot fired. I turned to look at Tom, but he wasn't running by my side anymore. Jim had disappeared too. They were huddled on the floor, back down the track. As I ran to them, I saw that Tom had been hit in the leg. Jim had already torn off some of his shirt to stop the bleeding.

'Jim, we gotta go!' I said anxiously. 'Tom will be all right. That's his family, they'll take care of him.'

Jim looked up. He almost looked disappointed in me. 'Your friend has been shot, Huck. We gotta help him.'

At that moment, I felt heavier and more tired than I had since living in the cabin with Pap.

I knew Jim was right, but it didn't seem fair. Jim was going to lose his freedom for good. All because of Tom's silly games. I watched as Jim lifted Tom up and started walking slowly back to the farmhouse. I ran in front, waving my arms to stop Uncle Silas from firing any more shots.

Tom (who everyone still thought was Sid) was taken straight to bed and a messenger was sent to Aunt Polly back in St Petersburg, telling her that her nephew had been taken ill. When Sally saw that Jim had helped Tom, she insisted that he was given some proper food and drink. Uncle Silas wanted him tied up again, but they tied him up in the kitchen rather than the barn this time.

I knew it would only be a matter of time before Aunt Polly arrived and realised that I had been pretending to be dead, and pretending to be Tom. I couldn't imagine the world of trouble I was about to get in from her and Widow Douglas.

I was dozing with my head on the kitchen table when I saw Aunt Polly and Uncle Silas coming downstairs. I rubbed my eyes in disbelief as I saw Uncle Silas untying the knots around Jim's wrists. 'What's happening?' I asked, panicked, thinking they were about to take Jim off someplace.

'It's okay, Huck,' Aunt Polly said. 'Tom has explained everything.' She sat at the kitchen table and took my hand, kindly. 'First of all, I'm overjoyed to see you safe and well. Everyone in St Petersburg was just devastated when we thought you had been killed. It's the first time I ever saw Judge Thatcher in tears.'

I couldn't believe it. I didn't think anyone would miss me, except for Tom and old Widow Douglas maybe.

Aunt Polly continued. 'Second of all, Tom's not been honest with you. I'm sorry to tell you that Widow Douglas passed away a few weeks ago. She knew that Jim didn't want to be sold, so she put it in her will that he and his family should be set free. Tom knew this before he came to visit this farm. It was the biggest news in town.'

I looked at Jim. I'd never seen a face so full of joy. 'So, I'm a free man?' Jim asked, his eyes brimming with tears. Aunt Polly nodded.

'Tom just admitted he didn't say anything because he thought it would be more exciting to free a slave, rather than free a man who was already free,' Aunt Polly said.

I should have been mad at Tom, but I was just so happy for Jim. I was also feeling sad about Widow Douglas passing away, but mighty proud of her too, for freeing Jim and his family. She was one of the kindest souls in St Petersburg.

'Does that mean I'm going to be sent back to Pap?' I asked,

sniffing away the tears that had started falling from my eyes.

Aunt Polly shook her head. 'I'm afraid he hasn't been seen since the flood.'

At this, Jim put a hand on my shoulder. 'Your pap won't be troubling you no more, Huck,' he said. 'You remember that house in the river the day after the flood? That room I wouldn't let you go in?'

I screwed up my face, trying to remember. It had only been a few weeks, but so much had happened. 'Yeah, I remember.'

'Your pap was in there. I'm sorry for not telling you. I couldn't find the right words.' Jim said.

My head was starting to spin. I hadn't slept right in days. The world seemed to have turned on its head. Jim was free, and Pap was dead. 'So, what about me?' I asked.

Polly held my hand tighter. 'You can come home with me

and Tom. If that's what you want?' she smiled.

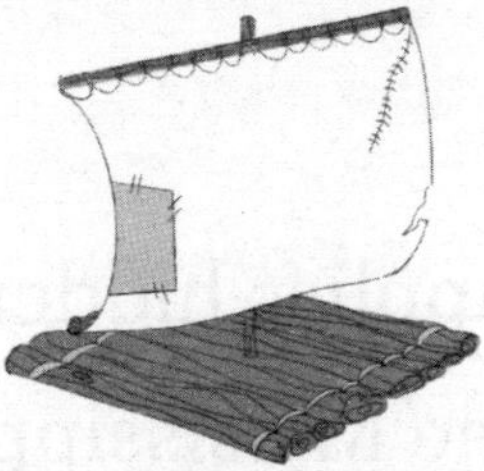

Epilogue

I saw Jim just one last time. He came to take his family away with him to the north, where they could make a real life for themselves. I like to picture them in a nice house, with Jim going off to work in the morning, coming home to his family every night.

I moved in with Tom, his brother Sid and Aunt Polly, and I even started liking school some, too. But I always keep a raft and a bag of supplies hidden by the banks of the Mississippi, just in case I ever need to go on another adventure.

Mark Twain

Mark Twain was born in Florida, USA in 1835. His real name was Samuel Langhorne Clemens, but he started writing under a pen name in the 1860s. His experiences growing up on the Mississippi River inspired many of his stories, including *The Adventures of Huckleberry Finn*. It is one of his most famous works and became a huge success when it was first published in 1884.